Dad Does It All

TREASURE BAY

Parent's Introduction

Welcome to **We Read Phonics**! This series is designed to help you assist your child in reading. Each book includes a story, as well as some simple word games to play with your child. The games focus on the phonics skills and sight words your child will use in reading the story.

Here are some recommendations for using this book with your child:

1 Word Play

There are word games both before and after the story. Make these games fun and playful. If your child becomes bored or frustrated, play a different game or take a break.

> Can you change the ending to make the word *dressing*?

Many of the games require printed materials (for example, sight word cards). You can print free game materials from your computer by going online to www.WeReadPhonics.com and clicking on the Game Materials link for this title. However, game materials can also be easily made with paper and a marker—and making them with your child can be a great learning activity.

② Read the Story

After some word play, read the story aloud to your child—or read the story together, by reading aloud at the same time or by taking turns. As you and your child read, move your finger under the words.

Next, have your child read the entire story to you while you follow along with your finger under the words. If there is some difficulty with a word, either help your child to sound it out or wait about five seconds and then say the word.

③ Discuss and Read Again

After reading the story, talk about it with your child. Ask questions like, "What happened in the story?" and "What was the best part?" It will be helpful for your child to read this story to you several times. Another great way for your child to practice is by reading the book to a younger sibling, a pet, or even a stuffed animal!

Dad, that's just like when you tried to do the wash!

Heh, heh. Well, I don't think your shirts came out quite that small.

LEVEL 6 Level 6 introduces words with "ey," "ie," and "y" with the long "e" sound (as in *key, chief,* and *sunny*), "oa," "oe," and "ow" with the long "o" sound (as in *boat, toe,* and *show*), and "ew" and "ue" with the long "u" sound (as in *crew* and *blue*). Also included are word endings -es, -ed, and -ly (as in *misses, started,* and *quickly*).

Dad Does It All

A We Read Phonics™ Book
Level 6

Text Copyright © 2011 by Treasure Bay, Inc.
Illustrations Copyright © 2011 by Jeffrey Ebbeler

Reading Consultants: Bruce Johnson, M.Ed., and Dorothy Taguchi, Ph.D.

We Read Phonics™ is a trademark of Treasure Bay, Inc.

Published by
Treasure Bay, Inc.
P.O. Box 119
Novato, CA 94948 USA

Printed in Singapore

Library of Congress Catalog Card Number: 2011925874

PDF E-Book ISBN: 978-1-60115-592-4
Hardcover ISBN: 978-1-60115-341-8
Paperback ISBN: 978-1-60115-342-5

We Read Phonics™
Patent Pending

Visit us online at:
www.TreasureBayBooks.com

PR-6-11

Dad Does It All

By Paul Orshoski
Illustrated by Jeffrey Ebbeler

Predicting Preview

Taking a careful look at the words in the story will help your child read those words or patterns.

om he made a cup of brew.
stuff was nasty = thick as gl

1. Take some standard Post-It notes. Cut into thin ¼ to ½ inch strips.

2. Go to a page in the book and choose a word. (This works best with a word on the last line of the page. Rhyming words are good to start with.)

3. Leave the first letter or set of sounds of the word uncovered, but cover the other letters with the Post-It note.

4. The child reads the page or sentence, and the first letter sound or sounds, and tries to predict the covered word.

For example: Turn to page 7. Choose the word *glue*. Leave the "gl" uncovered, but cover the "ue." The child reads the page and the first letter sound, and tries to predict what the covered word is.

Other words that work well include these words:

Page 9, milk

Page 10, bust

Page 11, nose

Page 12, pink

Page 16, mine

Page 24, time

Word Dominoes

Play this game to practice sight words used in the story.

Materials:

Option 1—Fast and Easy: To print free game materials from your computer, go online to www.WeReadPhonics.com, then go to this book title and click on the link to "View & Print: Game Materials."

Option 2—Make Your Own: With index cards and a marker or pen, make 10 word dominoes by placing each card horizontally and drawing a vertical line down the center. Write these words on the cards:

blue | yellow	yellow | our
our | pleased	pleased | soon
soon | worked	worked | out
out | they	they | saw
saw | some	some | blue

1. Spread out the dominoes face down. Turn one domino over.

2. Take turns picking a domino. If it matches a word on the first domino, say the word and place it so that the matching words are touching. If the selected domino doesn't match either of the words, put it back on the table face down, and the next player takes a turn. If scoring, keep track of how many dominoes each player is able to play.

My dad stayed home the other day.
My mom was sick. Her throat was gray.

When Mom is ill and feeling blue,
she lists the things that Dad must do.

Dad dressed up like a fancy maid.
He broke the eggs a chicken laid.

For Mom he made a cup of brew.
The stuff was nasty—thick as glue.

He gave the oatmeal too much heat.
The toast he burned was hard to eat.

He slipped on butter. Down he crashed!
He spilled the milk. His toe got mashed!

Dad started soon to clean and dust.
He smashed a vase. I saw it bust.

He ran the sweeper—crunched the hose.
But Mom kept snoring—out her nose.

My yellow socks, the two that stink,
he soaked them, and they came out pink.

He held my shirt and flashed a grin.
It came out tiny, small, and thin.

Then in the stove Dad put a roast.
He acted pleased. I saw him boast.

He said, "We need to let it stew."
We went outside—more jobs to do.

He hung some shirts out on the line.
They blew away—and some were mine!

Then as we chased them in the yard,
Dad said, "I never worked so hard."

When on the deck he sat to rest,
    a bird dropped droppings on his chest.

As Dad got up to wipe the slime,
the bird dropped slop a second time.

We went inside where something stunk.
Dad said, "I think I smell a skunk."

To Dad I said, "This is no joke.
Our supper just went up in smoke."

A haze went creeping down the hall.
I slipped away and made a call.

Dad threw our supper in the trash.
I told him, "Dad, I need some cash."

I waited for the bell to chime.
Our meal arrived here right on time.

The crust was thick. Each slice was hot.
That dinner really hit the spot!

Pair Power

Creating words from these vowel pairs will help your child reread this story.

Materials:

Option 1—Fast and Easy: To print free game materials from your computer, go online to www.WeReadPhonics.com, then go to this book title and click on the link to "View & Print: Game Materials."

Option 2—Make Your Own: You'll need paper or cardboard, scissors, and a crayon or marker. Cut out 30 cards that measure 2 x 2 inches. Then, make two consonant cards each of th, r, t, c, s, k, b, l, n, d, g, and f. Make three vowel-pair cards each of "oa" and "ew."

1. Deal four consonant cards to each player, and place the remaining cards face down on the table. Place the vowel-pair cards face down in a separate pile. Turn over the top vowel-pair card and place it on the table.

2. The first player tries to make a word by adding one or more of his consonant cards to the vowel pair. For example, if "oa" is on the table, adding "t" could make *oat.* The player receives one point for each letter added. If no word can be made, the player draws a consonant card and play continues until he can build a word.

3. After a word has been made, the next player tries to make a new word by adding one of her cards to the beginning or the end (for example by adding "c" to *oat* to make *coat*). If she can make a new word, she gets a new-word bonus point plus one point for each additional letter.

4. When no more letters can be played on the word, set aside the word. Turn over a new vowel-pair card, and the other player tries to make a new word.

5. Play continues until all of the vowel-pair cards have been used.

Great Endings

Creating words with certain endings will help your child reread this story, or read words with these endings in another story.

Materials:

Option 1—Fast and Easy: To print free game materials from your computer, go online to www.WeReadPhonics.com, then go to this book title and click on the link to "View & Print: Game Materials."

Option 2—Make Your Own: With thick paper or cardboard, index cards, scissors, and a pencil, crayon, or marker, cut five 2 x 2 inch squares from the paper or cardboard and print these ending letters and letter combinations on the squares: **er, ing, ed, es, s.** Print these twelve words on index cards (or on 2 x 4 inch pieces of paper): **dress, mail, scorch, spill, crack, start, crunch, drench, turn, soak, act, work**.

1 Ask your child to choose a word card. Then take the ending cards to make and say new words. For example, your child could choose the word "start" and the ending "ed". Put the cards together to make the new word *started*.

2 If needed, you can present the card "start" and ask your child to make *started*. You can also ask your child to change the ending to make the word *starting*.

3 Try to make as many words with these cards as possible.

27

If you liked *Dad Does It All,*
here is another **We Read Phonics** book you are sure to enjoy!

The Juggle Puzzle

Dean can juggle a tiger, a goat and a pot of stew! He is good at juggling, but when he has to cross a river, he has to solve a puzzle. How can he get them all across without the tiger eating the goat or the goat eating the stew?